Milly-
Molly-
Mandy
& Co

Milly-Molly-Mandy & Co

Joyce Lankester Brisley

MACMILLAN CHILDREN'S BOOKS

First published by George G. Harrap 1955

This edition published 2019 by Macmillan Children's Books
an imprint of Pan Macmillan
20 New Wharf Road, London N1 9RR
Associated companies throughout the world
www.panmacmillan.com

ISBN 978-1-5290-1065-7

Pan Macmillan does not have any control over, or any responsibility for,
any author or third-party websites referred to in or on this book.

3 5 7 9 8 6 4 2

A CIP catalogue record for this book is available from
the British Library.

Typeset by The Dimpse
Printed and bound by CPI Group (UK) Ltd, Croydon CR0 4YY

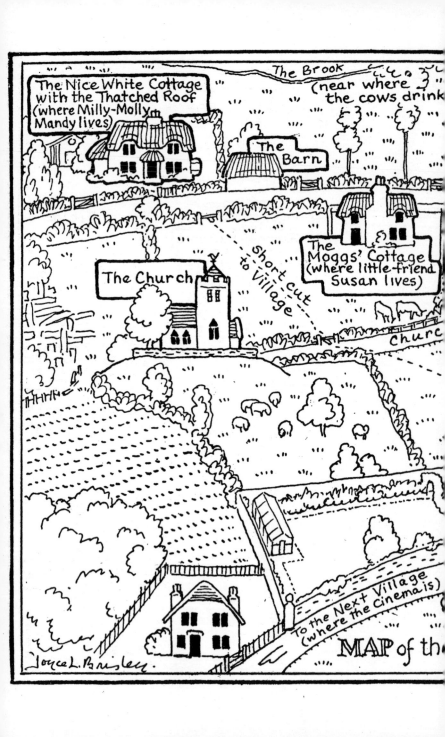

Contents

1

Milly-Molly-Mandy
Dresses Up

Once upon a time Milly-
Molly-Mandy found an old
skirt. She and little-friend-
Susan were playing up in
the attic of the nice white
cottage with the thatched
roof (where Milly-Molly-
Mandy lived). They had
turned out the rag-
bags and dressed
themselves in all sorts
of things – blouses

with the sleeves cut off, worn-out curtains, old nightgowns and shirts, and some of Milly-Molly-Mandy's own outgrown frocks (which Mother kept for patching her present ones, when needed).

Milly-Molly-Mandy and little-friend-Susan looked awfully funny – especially when they tried to put on the things which Milly-Molly-Mandy had outgrown. They laughed and laughed.

(The attic was rather a nice place for laughing in – it sort of echoed.)

Well, when Milly-Molly-Mandy found the old skirt of Mother's, of course she put it on. The waist had to fasten round her chest to make it short enough, but that didn't matter. She put on over it an old jumper with a burnt place in front, but she wore it back to front; so that didn't matter either.

Milly-Molly-Mandy walked up and down the attic, feeling just like Mother. She even wore a little brass curtain-ring on the finger of her left hand like Mother.

And then she had an idea.

"Let's both dress up and be ladies," said Milly-Molly-Mandy.

"Ooh, yes, let's," said little-friend-Susan.

So they picked out things from the rag-bags as best they could, and little-friend-Susan put on a dress which was quite good in front, only it had no back. She pulled her curls up on to the top of her head and tied them there with a bit of ribbon.

"LET'S BOTH DRESS UP AND BE LADIES"

Milly-Molly-Mandy tucked her hair behind her ears and fastened it behind with a bit of string, so that it made a funny sort of bun.

"We ought to wear coats and hats," said Milly-Molly-Mandy, "then we'd look quite all right."

So they went downstairs in their long skirts, and Milly-Molly-Mandy took Aunty's mackintosh from the pegs by the kitchen door for little-friend-Susan, and she borrowed an old jacket of Mother's for herself. They borrowed their hats too (not their best ones, of course), and went up to Mother's room to look in the mirror. They trimmed themselves up a bit from the rag-bags, and admired each other, and strutted about, enjoying themselves like anything.

And just then Mother called up the stairs: "Milly-Molly-Mandy?"

"Yes, Mother?" Milly-Molly-Mandy called down the stairs.

"When you go out, Milly-Molly-Mandy, please go to the grocer's and get me a tin of treacle. I shall be wanting some for making gingerbread. I've put the money on the bottom stair here."

So Milly-Molly-Mandy said: "Yes, Mother. I'll just go, Mother."

And then Milly-Molly-Mandy looked at little-friend-Susan. And little-friend-Susan looked at Milly-Molly-Mandy. And they said to each other, both at the same time:

"DARE you to go and get it like this!"

"Ooh!" said Milly-Molly-Mandy; and "Ooh!" said little-friend-Susan. "*Dare* we?"

"I'd have to tuck up my sleeves – they're too long," said Milly-Molly-Mandy. "Tell you what, Susan, we might go by the fields instead of down the road; then we wouldn't meet so many people. Look, I'll carry a shopping-basket, and you can take an umbrella, because it's easier when you've got something to carry. Come on."

So Milly-Molly-Mandy and little-friend-Susan crept downstairs and out at the front door, so that Father and Mother and Grandpa and Grandma and Uncle and Aunty mightn't see them. And they went down the front path to the gate.

But there was a horse and cart clip-clopping along the road, so they hung back and waited till it went by. And what do you think? The man driving it saw someone's back-view behind the gate, and he must have taken for granted it was Mother or Aunty or Grandma, for he called out, "Morning, ma'am!" as he passed.

Milly-Molly-Mandy and little-friend-Susan were so pleased they laughed till they had to hold each other up. But it made them feel much better.

They straightened their hats and hitched their skirts, and then they opened the gate and walked boldly across the road to the stile in the hedge on the other side.

It was quite a business getting over that stile. Milly-Molly-Mandy and little-friend-

Susan had to rearrange themselves carefully again on the other side.

Then, with their basket and umbrella, the two ladies set off along the narrow path across the field.

"Now, we mustn't laugh," said Milly-Molly-Mandy. "Ladies don't laugh a lot, not

outdoors. We shall give ourselves away if we keep laughing."

"No," said little-friend-Susan, "we mustn't. But suppose we meet Billy Blunt?"

"We mustn't run, either," said Milly-Molly-Mandy. "Ladies don't run much."

"No," said little-friend-Susan, "we mustn't. But I do hope we don't meet Billy Blunt."

"So do I," said Milly-Molly-Mandy. "I'd like to meet him worst of anybody. He'd be sure to know us. We mustn't keep looking round, either, Susan. Ladies don't keep on looking round."

"I was only wondering if anyone could see us," said little-friend-Susan.

But there were only cows on the far side of the meadow, and they weren't at all interested in the two rather short ladies walking along the narrow path.

Soon Milly-Molly-Mandy and little-friend-Susan came to the stile into Church Lane. This was a rather high stile, and while she was getting over it the band of Milly-Molly-Mandy's skirt slipped from her chest to her waist, and her feet got tangled in the length of it. She came down on all fours into the grass at the side, with her hat over one eye. But, luckily, she just got

straightened up before they saw the old gardener-man who looked after the churchyard coming along up the lane with his wheelbarrow.

"Let's wait till he's gone," said Milly-Molly-Mandy. "We'll be looking in my basket, so we needn't look up."

So they rummaged in the basket (which held only a bit of paper with the money in it), and talked in ladylike tones, until the old gardener-man had passed by.

He stared rather, and looked back at them once, but the two ladies were too busy to notice him.

When he was safely through the church-yard gate they went down the lane till they came to the forge at the bottom. Mr Rudge the Blacksmith was banging away on his anvil. He was a nice man, and Milly-Molly-Mandy and little-friend-Susan thought it would be fun to stop and see what he thought of them. So they stood at the doorway and watched him hammering at a piece of red-hot iron he was holding with his tongs.

Mr Rudge glanced up at them. And then he looked down. And then he went on hammering. And then he turned and put the piece of iron into the furnace. And while he worked the handle of the big bellows slowly up and down (to make the fire burn hot) he looked at them again over his shoulder, and said:

"Good morning, ladies. It's a warm day today."

"Yes, it is," agreed Milly-Molly-Mandy and little-friend-Susan. (They were feeling very warm indeed, though it wasn't at all sunny out.)

"Visitors in these parts, I take it," said the Blacksmith.

"Yes, we are," agreed Milly-Molly-Mandy and little-friend-Susan.

Then Milly-Molly-Mandy said: "Can you tell us if there is a good grocer's shop anywhere round here?"

"Let me see, now," said the Blacksmith, thinking hard. "Yes, I believe there is. Try going to the end of this lane, here, and turn sharp right – very sharp, mind. Then look both ways at once, and cross the road. You'll maybe see one."

Then he took his iron out, all red-hot, and began hammering at it again to shape it.

Milly-Molly-Mandy and little-friend-Susan couldn't be quite sure whether Mr Rudge knew them or not. They were just thinking of going on when – *who* should come round the corner of Mr Blunt's corn-shop but Billy Blunt himself!

Billy Blunt noticed the two rather odd-looking ladies standing in front of the forge. And he noticed one of them pull the other's sleeve, which came right down over her hand. And then they both turned and walked up the lane.

He thought they looked a bit queer somehow – short and rather crumpled. So he stopped at the forge and asked the Blacksmith:

"Who are those two?"

"Lady-friends of mine," said the Blacksmith, turning the iron and getting hold of it in a different place. "Lady-friends. Known 'em for years."

Billy Blunt waited, but the Blacksmith didn't say anything more. So he began strolling up the lane after the two ladies, who were near the stile by now.

The lady in the mackintosh seemed to be a bit flustered, whispering to the other. Then the other one said (so that he could hear):

"I seem to have lost my shopping-list, it isn't in my basket. Have you got it, dear?"

Billy Blunt strolled nearer. He wanted to see their faces.

"No, I haven't got it," said the first one. "We'd better go home and look for it. Oh, dear, I think it's coming on to rain. I felt a little spit. I must put up my umbrella."

And she opened it and held it over them both, so that Billy Blunt couldn't see so much of them.

He strolled a bit nearer, and stopped to pick an unripe blackberry from the hedge and put it in his mouth. He wanted to see the ladies climb over the stile.

But they waited there, rummaging in their basket and talking of the rain. Billy

17

Blunt couldn't feel any rain. Presently he heard the lady with the basket say in a rather pointed way: "I wonder what that *little boy* thinks he's doing there? He ought to go home."

And, quite suddenly, that's what the "little boy" did. At any rate he hurried off down the lane and out of sight.

Then Milly-Molly-Mandy and little-friend-Susan, very relieved, picked up their skirts and scrambled over the stile, and set off back across the fields. There was nobody to see them now but the cows, so they ran, laughing and giggling and tumbling against each other among the buttercups all the way across.

And by the time they got back to the first stile, just opposite the nice white cottage with the thatched roof (where Milly-Molly-Mandy lived), you never saw such a funny-looking pair of ladies!

Little-friend-Susan's hat-trimming had come off, and Milly-Molly-Mandy had stepped right out of her rag-bag skirt after it had tripped her up three times, and they were both so out of breath with giggling that they could hardly climb over on to the road.

But the moment they landed on the other side somebody jumped out at them from the hedge. And WHO do you suppose it was?

Yes, of course! It was Billy Blunt.

He had run all the way round by the road, just for the fun of facing them as they came across that stile.

"Huh! Think I didn't know you?" he asked, breathing hard. "I knew you at once."

"Then why didn't you speak to us?" asked little-friend-Susan.

"Think I'd want to speak to either of you looking like that?" said Billy Blunt, grinning.

"I don't believe you did know us, not just at once," said Milly-Molly-Mandy, "or you'd have said something, even if it was rude!"

"Look!" said little-friend-Susan. "There's someone coming. Let's go in quick!"

So they scurried across the road and through the garden gate. And just then Milly-Molly-Mandy's mother came out to pick a handful of flowers for the table.

"Well, goodness me!" said Mother. "Whatever's all this?"

"We were just dressing up," said Milly-Molly-Mandy, "when you wanted us to go to the village—"

"And we dared each other to go like this—" said little-friend-Susan.

"I saw the two ladies talking to the Blacksmith—" said Billy Blunt.

"Anyhow," said Milly-Molly-Mandy,

hopping on each leg in turn, her rag-bag hat-trimming looping over one eye, "we did dare, didn't we, Susan?"

"Well, well!" said Mother. "And where's my tin of treacle?"

Milly-Molly-Mandy stopped.

"We forgot all about it! I'm sorry, Mother. We'll go now!"

"Not like that!" said Mother. "You take my coat off, and go in and tidy yourselves first. And the attic too."

"I'll run and get the treacle for you," said Billy Blunt. "'Spect I stopped 'em – they'd got almost as far as the grocer's, anyhow."

"Yes, he scared us!" said Milly-Molly-Mandy, handing him Mother's money out of the basket. "He followed us along and never said a word. He thought we were proper ladies, that's why!"

"Thought you were proper guys," said Billy Blunt, going out of the gate.

2

Milly-Molly-Mandy Goes for a Picnic

Once upon a time Milly-Molly-Mandy was going for a picnic.

It was a real, proper picnic. Father and Mother and Uncle and Aunty were all going too, and little-friend-Susan and Billy Blunt (because it wouldn't seem quite a real, proper picnic without little-friend-Susan and Billy Blunt).

They were going to take the red bus from the cross-roads to a specially nice picnic place, where Milly-Molly-Mandy hadn't ever been before because it was quite a

MILLY-MOLLY-MANDY WAS GOING FOR A PICNIC

long way off. (The nicest places often do seem to be quite a long way off, somehow.)

Grandpa and Grandma weren't going. They said they would rather stay at home in the nice white cottage with the thatched roof, and keep house and milk the cows if the picnickers weren't back in time.

It was a quiet, misty sort of morning, which looked as if it meant to turn out a fine hot day, as Father and Mother and Uncle and Aunty and Milly-Molly-Mandy (and Toby the dog) set off down the road to the village, carrying the picnic things.

When they came to the Moggs' cottage little-friend-Susan (in a clean cotton frock) was ready and waiting for them at the gate.

And when they came to Mr Blunt's corn-

shop Billy Blunt (in a new
khaki shirt with pockets)
was ready and waiting for
them by the side-door.

And when they came to
the cross-roads the red bus
was already at the bus-stop.
And as, of course, it wouldn't wait long for
them, they all had to run like anything. But
they just caught it, and climbed inside.

Father took the tickets.

Let's see: Father and Mother and Uncle
and Aunty – that's four grown-up tickets.
And little-friend-Susan and Billy Blunt
and Milly-Molly-Mandy – that's three
half-tickets. (Father had asked the bus-
conductor as they got on, "Do you mind

the dog?" And the bus-conductor didn't, so Toby rode under the seat for nothing.)

Milly-Molly-Mandy said to little-friend-Susan and Billy Blunt as the bus went rattling along: "You haven't been to this place before, have you?" (hoping they hadn't).

Billy Blunt said: "Once. But I don't remember it. I was young then."

Little-friend-Susan said: "No. But my father and mother went a long time ago, and they say it's a nice place, and there's a wishing-well there, and you can drop a pin in and wish."

Billy Blunt said: "Don't believe in wishing-wells. Can't make things come true. Not if they aren't really."

And Milly-Molly-Mandy said: "Oh,

neither do I. But it's fun to pretend!"

And little-friend-Susan thought so too.

When they came to the next village (where the bus turned round ready to go back again) they all had to get out and walk. Father and Mother and Uncle and Aunty walked in twos, and Milly-Molly-Mandy and little-friend-Susan and Billy Blunt walked all in a bunch. And Toby the dog ran here and there, snorting into holes and getting his nose muddy. (He did enjoy it!)

The sun shone hot now, and they began to get quite thirsty. But Mother said: "We're nearly there, and then you can have a nice drink at the well!" And Aunty gave them some fruit-sweets wrapped in coloured papers.

Milly-Molly-Mandy and little-friend-Susan put their sweet-wrappers into their baskets, and Billy Blunt put his into one of his shirt pockets, to throw away when they got home.

Father said: "Well, anyone can see you've been properly brought up!"

He wished everyone who used that path did the same. He kept poking other people's bits of sweet-paper and orange-peel into the hedge with his stick as he went along, because they made the path look so nasty.

Mother said: "I think a place ought to look nicer because we've been there, not nastier!"

And Milly-Molly-Mandy and little-friend-Susan thought the same. Billy Blunt found a stick, and helped to poke the litter away too.

At last they came to the specially nice picnic place. And it really was almost like a fairy glen, with daisies and buttercups, and grassy slopes, and trees to climb, and a little stream running through the middle.

But – other people must have been there for picnics too, for – would you believe it? – they had left paper bags and egg-shells and litter everywhere. (And it almost spoiled everywhere, I can tell you.)

"Oh, dear!" said Father and Mother and Uncle and Aunty, looking all about.

"Where's the wishing-well?" asked Milly-Molly-Mandy and little-friend-Susan and Billy Blunt, looking all about too.

Father led the way to where some big, old trees were stooping round as if trying to hide something. And in behind them Milly-Molly-Mandy and little-friend-Susan and Billy Blunt saw a deep round hole in a wet rock which was simply covered over with beautiful green ferns and moss. And water, sparkling like crystal and cold as ice, was dripping down into it over the mossy rocks at the back.

It really did look just like a wishing-well!

Milly-Molly-Mandy and little-friend-Susan and Billy Blunt leaned over to see if they could see any pins lying at the bottom.

But – other people must have been there

too, and – would you believe it? – they had thrown in old tins and ice-cream cartons and litter, and there it was all lying under the water that was clear as crystal and cold as ice.

"Oh, *dear*!" said Milly-Molly-Mandy and little-friend-Susan and Billy Blunt. "Oh, dear; oh, dear!"

For you couldn't think of dropping a pin in and wishing there. You couldn't even have a drink.

Then Father said: "Mates, there's a spot of work to be done around here. We'd better get busy."

And he fished up some rusty tins out of the well with his stick.

Then Billy Blunt fished out some wet

papers and cartons with his stick. And Milly-Molly-Mandy and little-friend-Susan picked up bits of silver-paper and bus-tickets scattered about. And Father buried it all down a hole under a rock, where it couldn't be seen.

The well didn't look clear now, but Father said it would soon settle and be crystal clear again, as a wishing-well should be. So they thought they had better wait before making their wishes.

Meantime Mother and Aunty had chosen the best spot for the picnic, so Milly-Molly-Mandy and little-friend-Susan and Billy Blunt got busy collecting all the scraps of paper lying about, and Uncle put a match to them. (He took good care to do it where nothing else could catch fire or hurt the growing things, because, of course, when you have roots like trees and plants you can't move out of the way when you're getting hurt!) Billy Blunt collected bits of broken glass too, lest Toby the dog should cut his paws, and Father buried it safely.

By then it was time for the picnic, so they all washed their hands in the little stream running through the middle, and sat down to enjoy themselves.

They had hard-boiled eggs, and brown bread-and-butter, and cheese, and tomatoes, and buns and a big jam-tart. And to drink there was hot tea from a Thermos for the grown-ups, and cold milk for the young ones. And they were all so thirsty they drank

up every drop. (Toby the dog drank all he wanted from the little stream.)

When everyone had quite done they packed everything tidily away in their baskets to take home with them, all their empty bottles and wrapping-papers and string.

And then Father gave a great sigh of satisfaction, and lay back in the sunshine and put his hat over his face. And Mother sat in the shade and took up her knitting. And Uncle pulled out his newspaper with the cross-word puzzle. And Aunty opened her nice new lady's magazine.

But Milly-Molly-Mandy and little-friend-Susan and Billy Blunt (and Toby the dog) all wanted to be up and doing. So they ran about, paddling in the little stream and climbing the trees and playing hide-and-seek. And wherever they went they tidied up until there wasn't a bit of litter to be seen.

"Well!" said Milly-Molly-Mandy, looking about when it was almost time to go. "This picnic place looks ever so much nicer now *we've* visited it! I should think the next people would be pleased."

"I wish," said little-friend-Susan, "everybody would leave nice places nice when they visit them."

That made Billy Blunt remember something. And he said:

"We never made our wishes at the wishing-well."

So they all three rushed over to the wishing-well. And there it was, clear as crystal and cold as ice right down to the bottom, as a wishing-well should be. Mother gave them a cup, and they all drank, and filled up their bottle.

"Dropping just a pin in won't spoil it now, will it?" said Milly-Molly-Mandy.

"We can't make a proper wish without a pin," said little-friend-Susan.

"Won't make any difference anyhow," said Billy Blunt.

But he looked a bit disappointed, all the same, when Mother could find only two pins, which she gave to Milly-Molly-Mandy and little-friend-Susan. But then Father found one under his coat lapel, and handed it to Billy Blunt. And Billy Blunt looked quite pleased as he took it!

So they each dropped a pin into the wishing-well, and solemnly wished.

They couldn't tell their wishes out loud, because that might have spoiled the magic! But I *think* they all wished the same wish. And as Father said, if enough people wish a wish, and it's a *good* wish, it's quite likely to come to pass.

So let's hope that Milly-Molly-Mandy's and little-friend-Susan's and Billy Blunt's wishes all come true!

3

Milly-Molly-Mandy
Has a Clean Frock

Once upon a time, one beautiful, fine morning, Milly-Molly-Mandy came out in a nice clean frock. (Not for any special reason; only, of course, you have to have a clean frock sometimes, and a beautiful, fine morning seems a good enough reason.)

It was a Monday morning, so Mother was busy with the washing. Milly-Molly-Mandy helped her to get out the tin baths, and put up the washing-lines in the garden, and find the clothes-pegs. For with Father and Grandpa and Grandma and Uncle and

Aunty and Milly-Molly-Mandy and herself to wash for, Mother always had quite a busy time on Monday mornings.

"Well, now I think that will do, thank you, Milly-Molly-Mandy," said Mother at last. "You can run off and play now."

So Milly-Molly-Mandy called Toby the dog, and they went skipping off together in the beautiful sunshine, down the road with the hedges each side, to see if little-friend-Susan or Billy Blunt were coming out to play. She had only gone as far as the big meadow gate when whom did

she see but Billy Blunt (in a nice clean shirt), coming walking along up from the village. So Milly-Molly-Mandy waved hard and called out:

"Hullo, Billy! Where are you going?"

Billy Blunt just came walking on till he got near enough (so that he needn't bother

to shout), and then he held up an empty jam-jar he was carrying and said:

"Tadpoles."

"Oh!" said Milly-Molly-Mandy. "Where are you going to get them? What are you going to do with them? Can I come and help you?"

Billy Blunt said:

"I want to watch them turn into frogs in our water-butt."

Milly-Molly-Mandy said:

"There's tadpoles sometimes in the pond where the cows drink."

"I know," said Billy Blunt. "That's where I'm going. Come on."

So they climbed over the top bar of the big meadow gate, and Toby the dog squeezed under the bottom bar, and they walked along a narrow little path till they came to the pond where the cows drank.

Toby the dog ran off at once to the steep part to look for water-rats. Billy Blunt and Milly-Molly-Mandy walked round to the shallow part to look for tadpoles. But the pond was getting very low, and it was very muddy and trampled there. They couldn't get close without mud coming right over their shoes.

After a while they heard Toby the dog barking excitedly, because he had found a rat-hole and wanted the owner to come out and be caught. (As if any sensible rat would!) But presently the barking turned to a splashing and yelping, so Milly-Molly-Mandy and Billy Blunt ran along the bank to see what had happened.

And – goodness me! – somehow or other Toby the dog must have slipped over the edge, for there he was, right in the pond. And he *was* in a mess! – all covered with mud and weedy stuff.

"He can't climb out there – it's too steep," said Billy Blunt. And he called, "Come on, Toby!" and tried to lead him along to where the bank was lower.

But Toby the dog just kept trying to scramble out where he had slipped in.

"He can't swim through that mud and weedy stuff, that's why," said Milly-Molly-Mandy. And she reached down to try to pull him out. But she just couldn't get him, so she reached over farther.

And then – goodness me! – somehow or other she must have reached over too far, for next moment there was Milly-Molly-Mandy in the pond too. And she *was* in a mess! – all covered with moss and weedy stuff.

Billy Blunt said: "Well! Of all the cuckoos!" And he reached down to try to pull her out.

Milly-Molly-Mandy said: "Let's get Toby out first."

So they got Toby the dog out on to the bank. And directly he found himself there Toby the dog shook himself violently, and mud and weedy stuff flew out all round, right over Billy Blunt's clean shirt.

Billy Blunt stepped back in a hurry.

And then – goodness me! – somehow or other he must have stepped over the edge of the bank, for next moment there was Billy Blunt in the pond now (nearly on top of Milly-Molly-Mandy). And he *was* in a mess! – all covered with mud and weedy stuff. (Milly-Molly-Mandy might have said:

"Well! Of all the cuckoos!" But she was really too busy just then.)

The pond wasn't deep, and they were able to scramble out all right. But – goodness me! – you NEVER did see such a mess as Milly-Molly-Mandy and Billy Blunt and Toby the dog were in! – all covered with mud and weedy stuff.

"Oh, dear!" said Milly-Molly-Mandy. "Now what shall we do?"

"Umm," said Billy Blunt. "What will my mother say?"

"Will she be very cross?" asked Milly-Molly-Mandy. "You couldn't help it."

Billy Blunt only said: "It was a clean shirt." And he tried to squeeze the water out of it.

Milly-Molly-Mandy said: "My dress was

clean too." And she tried to squeeze the water out of it.

But the more they squeezed the worse things seemed to get.

"We'd better go home," said Billy Blunt at last.

"Let's go to my home first," said Milly-

Molly-Mandy. "P'raps Mother will know what to do before your mother sees you."

Billy Blunt said: "Well – I suppose I'd better see you get home all right, anyhow."

So they went across the fields and through two hedges, instead of by the road (so that nobody should see them). And they crept through the back gate into the garden of the nice white cottage with the thatched roof (where Milly-Molly-Mandy lived).

Mother was busy hanging sheets out on the line, and she didn't notice them at first.

So Milly-Molly-Mandy said: "Mother—" (but not very loudly).

And Mother turned round. And she saw them standing there, Milly-Molly-Mandy,

Billy Blunt and Toby the dog, all covered with mud and weedy stuff.

"OH!" said Mother

"We fell in the cow-pond," said Milly-Molly-Mandy in a small voice. "Toby fell in first and I tried to get him out and I fell in and Billy tried to get me out and he fell in and – we're very sorry, Mother."

And Billy Blunt nodded.

"Oh!" said Mother again.

And then she said: "Stay there!"

And she went indoors.

So Milly-Molly-Mandy and Billy Blunt and Toby the dog stayed there, wondering what Mother meant to do with them, and if she were very cross. Milly-Molly-Mandy wanted to wipe the mud off her face, but her hand was too dirty. Billy Blunt wanted to blow his nose, but his handkerchief was too wet. Toby the dog rolled in the dust to dry himself. (But it didn't make him look better.)

When Mother came out again she was carrying the tin bath she used for the washing, and after her came Aunty carrying the tin bath used for the rinsing, and they set them down on the grass. Then they went indoors and came out again, Mother with a big kettle and some soapflakes, Aunty with a big bucket and some towels. When they had put warm water in the two tin baths, Mother emptied the whole packet of soapflakes in and swished around with her hand in each till the bubbles rose up, and up, and UP.

Then Mother took Milly-Molly-Mandy, and Aunty took Billy Blunt, and they peeled the clothes off them and plopped them, into the two tin baths then and there!

"Now!" said Mother. "Get busy and clean yourselves."

And she gathered up the dirty clothes into the bucket and pumped water over them at the pump.

So there were Milly-Molly-Mandy and Billy Blunt that beautiful fine morning, each in a bathful of warm bubbles nearly up to their necks, with the sheets flapping round them, and the sun shining, and the birds singing.

Then they got busy, swishing about in their baths, making more and yet more

GOODNESS ME! THOSE WERE NICE BATHS

bubbles. They lathered
their heads till they
looked as if they had
curly white hair and
beards. They blew
great coloured
bubbles between

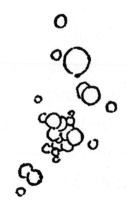

their hands and watched them float off
into the sky. They threw handfuls of
bubbles at Toby the dog, which he tried
to catch as the wind carried them away
between the clothes that Mother and
Aunty were pegging up on the clothes-
lines.

Soon Milly-Molly-Mandy and Billy
Blunt were really enjoying themselves
like anything, laughing and shouting, with

Toby the dog barking and the sun shining and the birds singing.

Goodness me! Those were nice baths!

And you can't think how *clean* they both felt when at last Mother made Milly-Molly-Mandy get out into a big towel and hurried her indoors to put something dry on, and Billy Blunt got out into another big towel and Mother lent him some pyjamas of Father's to put on.

Then Mother washed their clothes in one of the baths and Aunty caught Toby the dog and washed him in the other. And then they threw the water out and washed the baths!

Then Milly-Molly-Mandy came out in a dressing-gown (because both her dresses were in the wash), and she and Billy Blunt, in big pyjamas, sat in the sun together, drying their hair and eating biscuits while their clothes flapped on the line and Toby the dog rolled in dust to get the cleanness off him. (He was the only one who didn't enjoy his bath.)

Mother quickly ironed up Billy Blunt's shirt and shorts and Milly-Molly-Mandy's pink-and-white striped frock. And when they put them on again you would never dream what they had been up to that beautiful, fine morning.

"Well," said Milly-Molly-Mandy, "I am sorry we got so dirty, Mother, but I *did* like that bubble-bath!"

"Yes," said Billy Blunt. "I wouldn't care if I had to have a bubble-bath every day!"

But Mother said:

"Now listen, you two. Maybe you couldn't help it this time. But if you come home like that *again* you won't have bubble-baths! I shall put you in the cow-trough and turn the pump on you! This has been the biggest washing-day I've had, and I don't want another like it."

So then Billy Blunt said: "No, ma'am. I'm very much obliged to you, ma'am." And he thanked Aunty too.

Then he went off home in his nice clean things, sure that his mother would never dream what he had been up to.

But when Mrs Blunt saw him come in (rather late for dinner, but looking so clean and tidy) she guessed he had been up to *something*. And when she saw his muddy shoes, and found he hadn't caught any tadpoles and didn't know what he had done with his jam-jar, she pretty well guessed everything.

But Mrs Blunt never dreamed what grand

bubble-baths Billy Blunt and Milly-Molly-Mandy had had, out in the garden of the nice white cottage with the thatched roof that beautiful fine morning!

4

Milly-Molly-Mandy and the Golden Wedding

Once upon a time Milly-Molly-Mandy was busy dipping fingers of bread-and-butter into her boiled egg at supper-time, and listening while Father and Mother and Grandpa and Grandma and Uncle and Aunty talked.

They were counting how long it was that Grandpa and Grandma had been married. And it was a very long time indeed – nearly fifty years!

Grandma said: "Our Golden Wedding – next month!"

Milly-Molly-Mandy was very interested, though she did not know what a Golden Wedding was. But it sounded rather grand.

"Do you have to be married all over again when you've been married fifty years?" she asked.

"No," said Mother; "it's more like having a very special sort of birthday. When you've been married twenty-five years you have a Silver Wedding Day, and people give you silver presents. But when you've been married fifty years it's a Golden one.

We shall have to think what we can do to celebrate Grandpa's and Grandma's Golden Wedding Day. Dear me!"

Milly-Molly-Mandy whispered: "Do we have to give golden presents to Grandpa and Grandma?"

Mother whispered back: "We shall have to think what we can do about it, Milly-Molly-Mandy. But there are different sorts of gold, you know – sunshine and buttercups and, well, little girls, even, can be good as gold sometimes! We shall have to think."

Grandpa (eating his kipper) heard their whisperings, and said: "If Milly-Molly-Mandy promises to be as good as gold that day you can just wrap her up in tissue-paper and hand her over. She'll do for a Golden Wedding present!"

But Milly-Molly-Mandy wouldn't promise to be as good as all that!

She did wonder, though, what sort of gold presents Father and Mother and Uncle and Aunty would be giving to Grandpa and Grandma. And she wondered too, very much, what sort of a gold present she herself could give. It was important to think of something very special for such a special occasion.

She talked with little-friend-Susan and Billy Blunt about it before school next morning.

Little-friend-Susan said: "I'd like to give a present too. But I haven't enough money."

Billy Blunt said: "I'd be rich if I could give anybody a gold present!"

"But it doesn't always have to be that sort of present," Milly-Molly-Mandy told them. "There's good-as-gold, if we could think of something like that. Only I can't think what."

And then they met others on their way in to school, and had other things to think about.

A few days later Billy Blunt showed Milly-Molly-Mandy a crumpled bit of newspaper he had in his pocket, and made her read it. It was something about a golden-jubilee concert somewhere. Milly-Molly-Mandy couldn't think why Billy Blunt bothered to keep it.

"Plain as your nose," said Billy Blunt. "Golden jubilee means fifty years, like your Golden Wedding business. They're having a concert to celebrate. Thought you might be interested."

And then, suddenly, Milly-Molly-Mandy was very interested.

"You mean *we* might do something like that for Grandpa and Grandma? Oh, Billy! what a good idea. What can we do?"

But Billy Blunt only said: "Oh, it was just an idea."

And he went off to exchange foreign stamps with a friend of his, Timmy Biggs. So Milly-Molly-Mandy looked for little-friend-Susan to tell her.

"But what could we do for a concert?" asked little-friend-Susan. "We can't play or anything."

But Milly-Molly-Mandy said (like Mother): "We shall have to think, Susan!"

The Golden Wedding meant a lot of thinking for everybody – Father and Mother and Uncle and Aunty as well.

Mother had the first idea. She said (while Grandpa and Grandma were out of the way):

"I shall make a big golden wedding-cake, iced with yellow icing, and trimmed with gold hearts and a gold paper frill. We'll have a Golden Wedding tea-party!"

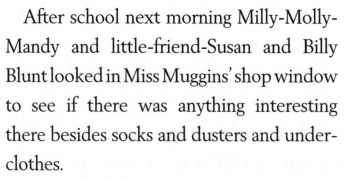

Father and Uncle and Aunty and Milly-Molly-Mandy thought that was a grand idea!

After school next morning Milly-Molly-Mandy and little-friend-Susan and Billy Blunt looked in Miss Muggins' shop window to see if there was anything interesting there besides socks and dusters and under-clothes.

"There's a little gold bell with a handle on that shelf – see," said Milly-Molly-Mandy, "and pins with gold heads."

"Those yellow pencils with gold tops look quite cheap," said little-friend-Susan, "and that Happy Returns card with gold print!"

(Really, there seemed quite a number of gold things if you kept your eyes open!)

Billy Blunt looked carefully, but said nothing.

"Have you thought what you can do at the concert?" Milly-Molly-Mandy asked him.

"What concert?" said Billy Blunt.

"Our Golden Wedding concert, of course!" said Milly-Molly-Mandy.

"Huh!" said Billy Blunt. And then he said: "Better call a meeting and make plans."

"Ooh, yes let's!" said Milly-Molly-Mandy and little-friend-Susan together. And

Milly-Molly-Mandy added, "Somewhere secret, where Grandpa and Grandma won't know!"

Billy Blunt said they might come to his place after tea on Saturday; his folk would be in the corn-shop, and they could plan in private there.

So directly after tea on Saturday Milly-Molly-Mandy met little-friend-Susan at the Moggs' gate, and they ran together down to the village, and through the gate at the side of the corn-shop, and up the garden path into the Blunts' house.

"Oh, it's you," said Billy Blunt (as if he wasn't expecting them).

Milly-Molly-Mandy hadn't seen inside the Blunts' sitting-room before, only in the corn-shop. It was small and rather dark, but very cosy, with a thick red cloth on the table.

"Sit down," said Billy Blunt. "The meeting's begun. I'm President, as it's my house."

"But it's *my* Golden Wedding," Milly-Molly-Mandy told him.

They laughed at that (because Milly-Molly-Mandy didn't look over fifty), and then they felt more at home.

Billy Blunt thumped on the table, and said, "Order, now!"

And they settled down to thinking what they could do about a concert.

They couldn't play the piano, though there was one which Aunty played on at the nice white cottage with the thatched roof (where, of course, Milly-Molly-Mandy lived). Billy Blunt had an old mouth-organ, but it was broken. And little-friend-Susan had a dulcimer, but her baby sister played with it and half the notes were gone.

"Then we'll have to make up things," said Milly-Molly-Mandy. "I can play a comb and tissue-paper!"

"Saucepan lids make awfully nice clappers," said little-friend-Susan.

Billy Blunt reached down and picked up the shovel and poker from the fireplace and started hitting them together, till Milly-Molly-Mandy and little-friend-Susan shouted at him that Grandpa and Grandma wouldn't like that one bit! So then he put the shovel to his shoulder and sawed

up and down
it with the
poker,
singing,
"Tweedle-
tweedle-
tweedle,"
exactly as if
he were playing
the violin!

Milly-Molly-Mandy and little-friend-Susan *did* wish they had thought of that first!

"Well!" said Milly-Molly-Mandy. "We can have a band, and then we'll recite something. What can we say?"

"Let's write a poem," said little-friend-Susan.

So they thought awhile. And then Milly-Molly-Mandy said:

*"Dear Grandpa and Grandma, we want to say
We wish you a happy Golden Wedding Day!"*

"Bit long," said Billy Blunt.

"But it rhymes," said Milly-Molly-Mandy.

"Yes, it does," said little-friend-Susan. "Can't we get in something about Many Happy Returns?"

"Can you have returns of Golden Weddings?" asked Milly-Molly-Mandy. "I thought you only had one."

"You could have one every fifty years, I expect," said Billy Blunt. "You'd be a bit old by next time, though!"

"Well, we'd like Grandpa and Grandma to have heaps of Golden Weddings, till they were millions of years old!" said Milly-Molly-Mandy.

So they thought again, and added:

"We want you to know our heart all burns.
To wish you Many Happy Returns."

Billy Blunt wrote it down on a piece of paper, and while the others tried to think up some more he went on scribbling for a bit. Then he read out loudly:

"We hope you like this little stunt,
Done by Mister William Blunt!"

There was a lot of shouting at that, as the others, of course, wanted to have their names in too! They made so much noise that Mrs Blunt looked in from the corn-shop to see what was up.

Billy Blunt said: "Sorry, Mum!" And they went on with the meeting in whispers.

Well, the great day arrived.

Only a few special people were invited to the party, but there seemed quite a crowd – Grandpa and Grandma, Father and Mother, Uncle and Aunty, Mr Moggs and Mrs Moggs (their nearest neighbours), little-friend-Susan and Baby Moggs (who couldn't be left behind), Billy Blunt (by special request), and, of course, Milly-Molly-Mandy.

Mother and Aunty between them had prepared a splendid tea, with the big decorated Golden Wedding cake in the centre, and buttered scones, and brown and white bread-and-butter and honey, and apricot jam, and lemon-curd tarts, and orange buns (everything as nearly golden-coloured as possible, of course) arranged round it.

But before Mother filled the teapot everybody had to give Grandpa and Grandma their golden presents. (Milly-Molly-Mandy and little-friend-Susan and Billy Blunt were all very interested to see what everyone was giving!)

Well, Mr and Mrs Moggs gave a beautiful

MOTHER AND AUNTY BETWEEN THEM HAD PREPARED A SPLENDID TEA

gilt basket tied with gold ribbons, full of lovely yellow chrysanthemums.

Father and Mother gave a pair of real gold cuff-links to Grandpa, and a little gold locket (with a photo of Milly-Molly-Mandy inside) to Grandma.

Uncle and Aunty gave a gold coin to hang on Grandpa's watch-chain, and a thin gold neck-chain for Grandma's locket.

And then it was time for Milly-Molly-Mandy and little-friend-Susan and Billy Blunt to give their presents.

They stood in a row, and Billy Blunt lifted his shovel-and-poker violin, and Milly-Molly-Mandy her comb-and-tissue-paper mouth-organ, and little-friend-Susan her saucepan-lid clappers; and they played and sang, hummed and clashed, *Happy Birthday to You!* only instead of "birthday" they sang, "Happy Golden Wedding to you!"

And then they shouted their own poem all together:

"Dear Grandpa and Grandma, we want to say
We wish you a happy Golden Wedding Day.
We want you to know our heart all burns
To wish you Many Happy Returns.
We hope you like our little stunt,
From Milly-Molly-Mandy, Susan, and Billy
*   Blunt!"*

Grandpa and Grandma were nearly overcome, and everybody clapped as the three gave their presents then: two long yellow pencils with brass ends (which looked like gold) from little-friend-Susan; two "Golden-Glamour Sachets" from Billy Blunt; and a little gold bell to ring whenever they wanted her from Milly-Molly-Mandy.

Grandpa and Grandma WERE pleased! There was quite a bit of talk over Billy Blunt's sachets, though, as he had thought they were scent sachets, but the others said they were shampoos for golden hair, and, of course Grandpa's and Grandma's hair was white!

However, Grandma said her sachet smelled so delicious she would keep it among her hand-kerchiefs, and Grandpa could do the same with his. So *that* was all right.

Then they had tea, and Grandpa and Grandma cut big slices of their Golden Wedding cake, with a shiny gilt heart for everybody.

Afterwards Grandpa made quite a long speech. But all Grandma could say was that she thought such a lovely Golden Wedding was well worth waiting fifty years for!

So then Milly-Molly-Mandy and little-friend-Susan and Billy Blunt knew they had really and truly helped in making it such a splendid occasion!

5

Milly-Molly-Mandy Cooks a Dinner

Once upon a time Milly-Molly-Mandy was coming home after morning school with little-friend-Susan and Billy Blunt.

They were all talking about what they might be going to have for their dinners (feeling very hungry at that time, of course), and about the sort of things they liked and the sort of things they didn't like.

Billy Blunt said he didn't like turnips or parsnips, and little-friend-Susan said she didn't like potatoes or carrots. Milly-Molly-Mandy said what she didn't like was stew, with bits of meat and vegetables floating in it. And Billy Blunt and little-friend-Susan agreed that that was just what they didn't like either. They all hoped none of them would have stew for dinner that day!

(They needn't have worried, for none of them did.)

The next day was Saturday, and there was no school. So Milly-Molly-Mandy stayed around the nice white cottage with the thatched roof, helping Father in the garden.

Father was very busy, digging up potatoes and cutting down dead plants and burning rubbish on a big bonfire. So Milly-Molly-Mandy was very busy too, sweeping up leaves and picking up tools which Father dropped and throwing bits on to the bonfire.

(Autumn is a very busy time in a garden.)

Presently little-friend-Susan came wandering up the road, wondering what Milly-Molly-Mandy was doing. She saw the smoke, so she peeped over the hedge outside the nice white cottage with the thatched roof.

"Hullo, Susan!" called Milly-Molly-Mandy. "Look at our bonfire! You'd better come and help me to help Father!"

So little-friend-Susan ran in at the gate and round to the back garden. And soon the two of them were very busy, throwing bits on to the bonfire.

Presently Billy Blunt came wandering up

the road, wondering (rather) what Milly-Molly-Mandy was doing. He saw the smoke too, and looked over the hedge outside the nice white cottage with the thatched roof. "Hullo, Billy!" called Milly-Molly-Mandy. "Look, it's a bonfire! Come and help us to help Father!"

So Billy Blunt walked in at the gate and round to the back garden. And soon all three of them were very busy throwing bits on to the bonfire.

(But somehow, Father thought, three people together weren't half so helpful as one person alone!)

The bonfire puffed big, beautiful clouds of smoke out, and, whichever side they stood it seemed trying to puff right into their faces. Milly-Molly-Mandy and little-friend-Susan and Billy Blunt had to keep running round to one side or another as they threw on bits of twig and dead leaves.

"Tell you what," said Billy Blunt, after a while, "if we had some chestnuts we could roast them."

But they hadn't any chestnuts so they couldn't.

"I wonder what else there is we could

cook," said Milly-Molly-Mandy, looking about.

And then she noticed a heap of straggly old bean-plants waiting to be burned, and they had a few big bean-pods still hanging on here and there.

"Oh look!" said Milly-Molly-Mandy; "perfectly good beans!"

"Can't we cook them?" said little-friend-Susan.

"You can't eat those," said Billy Blunt. "Too old."

"Maybe you can't eat them at the table," said Milly-Molly-Mandy, "but if we cook them ourselves on the bonfire maybe we could!"

So they all searched for bean-pods and

opened them, and they got quite a handful of lovely big purple-speckled beans.

"What do we cook them in?" said Milly-Molly-Mandy.

"They'll need a lot of boiling," said little-friend-Susan.

"You want a tin can, like tramps have!" said Billy Blunt.

That was a bright idea. So Milly-Molly-Mandy ran indoors to ask Mother, and Mother gave her an empty treacle-tin with a lid. They washed it well under the pump, and put the beans in with some clean water, and set it on the bonfire to boil. They had to watch it, because when the fire blazed up the tin fell over, and Billy Blunt had to rescue it with the gardening-fork. It boiled till the lid blew off. And then Billy Blunt (who was beginning to feel hungry) said:

"I should think they're done now."

So they emptied the tin out on to the ground and divided the beans. They were quite soft inside, so they peeled the skins off, and ate them rather like chestnuts. They did enjoy them!

When Father came along with another load of weeds and brambles to put on the bonfire and saw what they were doing, he said:

"Ah, if you want real gipsy cooking there's nothing to beat a good hot potato, baked in its jacket!" And he pointed to the wheelbarrow full of newly dug potatoes, and added, "Help yourselves – only don't waste them."

Milly-Molly-Mandy and little-friend-Susan and Billy Blunt *were* pleased! They helped themselves to two potatoes each, and Father showed how to bury them in the hot ashes under the bonfire.

"You'll have to leave them for a good half-hour and more," he said, as he went off.

It seemed an awfully long time to wait. They were all feeling very hungry by now.

"Tell you what," said Billy Blunt, "we ought to get some salt and butter to eat with those potatoes when they're done."

"Oo, yes!" said little-friend-Susan, "we ought."

"Let's ask Mother," said Milly-Molly-Mandy.

So they went into the kitchen, where Mother was putting a pie into the oven and Aunty was laying the table.

"Please," said Milly-Molly-Mandy, "could we have just a bit of butter and salt to eat with our baked potatoes out there?"

"Goodness me!" said Mother. "Whatever next?"

"They'll spoil their dinners next," said Aunty. "Oh, we won't – truly – we're so dreadfully hungry!" said Milly-Molly-Mandy. And little-friend-Susan and Billy Blunt said: "Yes, we are!"

"But dinner will be ready in half an hour," said Mother.

"Oh, dear – so will our potatoes be!" said Milly-Molly-Mandy.

"They're cooking under the bonfire," said little-friend-Susan.

"We're not to waste them," said Billy Blunt.

Then Milly-Molly-Mandy had a bright idea.

"Mother, couldn't you let us cook our own dinners all by ourselves out on the bonfire, just for once? It would be such fun! Please! Couldn't we, Mother?"

"*Yes*!" said little-friend-Susan and Billy Blunt.

"But what would your mothers say if you don't go home to a proper dinner?" Mother asked them.

"We could go and ask," said little-friend-Susan and Billy Blunt at once.

"Well," said Mother, "if Mrs Moggs and Mrs Blunt don't object I suppose you may, just this once."

So little-friend-Susan and Billy Blunt

rushed off to ask permission while Milly-Molly-Mandy borrowed a saucepan (one that didn't matter very much), and some old cooking-plates and spoons, and some bread, and salt, and butter (margarine really).

Mother gave her some scraps of meat, and told her to help herself to whichever vegetables she wanted from the box in the scullery. So Milly-Molly-Mandy helped herself to some of everything – onions, carrots, parsnips – and carried all outside in readiness.

Very soon little-friend-Susan came running back, saying her mother didn't mind if Milly-Molly-Mandy's mother didn't. And she brought a strip of bacon in a paper.

Then Billy Blunt came panting back

(he had farther to go), saying his mother made no objection if he chose to miss a proper dinner this once. And he brought a sausage on an old fork.

Father had made the bonfire burn up till it was mostly just a heap of red-hot ashes now.
Then he went indoors to have his dinner. And the three of them stayed outdoors, and got to work cooking their own.

Milly-Molly-Mandy cut up vegetables into the

saucepan, with scraps of meat and some water, and set it on top of the fire to boil. Little-friend-Susan toasted bacon on a stick. And Billy Blunt toasted sausage on a fork.

Then they remembered the potatoes, and Milly-Molly-Mandy started poking about in the ashes. Little-friend-Susan was so busy watching her that she let her bacon catch fire; and Billy Blunt was so busy grinning to see her blowing it out that he didn't notice his own sausage burning until the others shouted at him! After a good scraping the bit of bacon and the sausage were added to the stew to finish cooking while the potatoes were got out.

"Aren't they beautifully done!" said

Milly-Molly-Mandy, brushing their skins on the grass.

"Aren't they hot!" said little-friend-Susan, sucking her fingers.

"Let's begin!" said Billy Blunt.

So, as they were all frightfully hungry by now and the stew wasn't quite done, they each took a hot baked potato in their hands and broke it open, and put in a dab of butter and a pinch of salt, and ate it out of its skin – like that, standing round the bonfire.

And, my! you never tasted anything so good as those potatoes!

"It's made me hungrier than ever," said Billy Blunt, when he had eaten his two.

So then they couldn't wait any longer.

THEY EACH TOOK A HOT BAKED POTATO

They took the saucepan off the fire and spooned stew out on to the plates. It tasted rather of bonfire smoke, and they had forgotten the salt, and the vegetables were a bit hard.

But, my! you *never* tasted anything so good as that stew!

And, as Billy Blunt said, "It's good for your teeth to bite up well. Too much soft food's bad."

So they all bit up very well indeed, dividing everything equally down to the last scrap.

One thing is very certain, Grandma would have said that "Mr Manners" didn't get much of a look-in at that meal. (But then, you couldn't expect to find "Mr

Manners" anywhere around in so much bonfire smoke!)

"Well," said Milly-Molly-Mandy at last, "we can't say we don't like stew, or carrots, or potatoes, or parsnips now!"

"Ah," said Billy Blunt, "but we never have stew like this at home!"

"I wish," said little-friend-Susan, "we

could always cook our dinners ourselves. It would save a lot of washing up, too."

Just then Mother looked out of the back door.

"What about finishing up this treacle-tart, though you haven't cooked it yourselves?" she called.

Well, of course, you couldn't say no to Mother's treacle-tart. So they managed to find enough room, but only just! Then, sticky, greasy, smoky, and very comfortable inside, they carried their things indoors to be washed up.

But – do you know! – there seemed to be more washing up to be done than they had supposed. For, besides their plates and spoons and the saucepan, there were –

Milly-Molly-Mandy and little-friend-Susan and Billy Blunt!

(And they took a good deal of washing up, I can tell you!)

6

Milly-Molly-Mandy Acts for the Pictures

Once upon a time something quite exciting happened in the village where Milly-Molly-Mandy lived.
Anyhow, Milly-Molly-Mandy and little-friend-Susan and (I think) even Billy Blunt were quite excited over it.

Milly-Molly-Mandy was going

with little-friend-Susan on an errand to Miss Muggins' shop one morning. And they had just turned the corner by the duck-pond when they noticed rather a lot of people standing about, though there didn't seem much to see – only one or two cars and a sort of van-thing drawn up by the Inn.

"I wonder what's going on," said Milly-Molly-Mandy.

Little-friend-Susan wondered too. But they thought they had better get their shopping done first, before trying to find out.

As they passed the forge they didn't see the Blacksmith. And as they passed Mr Blunt's corn-shop they didn't see Billy Blunt. But Mrs Hubble was peeping through the window of her baker's shop, and a very big, shiny motor-car came sliding along past them on its way to the Inn.

Something certainly seemed to be going on. But they couldn't think what.

They went into Miss Muggins' draper's shop, and Miss Muggins came out of her inner room to serve them. (She had been to put the dinner on to cook – you could smell it.)

Little-friend-Susan said: "Two yards of narrow white elastic and a packet of mixed needles for Mother, please," and put her money on the counter.

And while Miss Muggins pulled out a drawer Milly-Molly-Mandy looked round and said: "Where's your Jilly, Miss

Muggins?" – because nobody seemed to be about. (Jilly, of course, was Miss Muggins' little niece who lived with her.)

Miss Muggins, winding up elastic very quickly between her thumb and little finger, said: "Jilly? Oh, she's over by the Inn, watching those film people taking movies there."

"MOVIES?"
said Milly-
Molly-
Mandy and
little-friend-
Susan,
loudly
and both
together.

"Didn't you know?" said Miss Muggins, wrapping up the elastic and the needles in thin brown paper. "They've been at it since early morning, up and down in their motor-cars. I don't know what they want to do it here for. Looks an ordinary enough place, to my way of thinking."

"Do you mean, they are making a film? Here? In our village?"

"So they say," said Miss Muggins, pulling open the drawer that went *ping!* under the counter, for little-friend-Susan's change. "Jilly's been hanging round, of course, ever since they arrived. She could hardly wait to eat her breakfast, and would have her hair done up in curl-papers last night."

"She's not going to act in the movie, is

she?" asked little-friend-Susan.

"If she can squeeze in front of the camera while no one's looking I shouldn't be surprised," said Miss Muggins. "She's quite crazy about films. If you see her remind her it'll be dinner-time soon. Tell her not to be late."

"Yes, Miss Muggins, we will. Hurry, Susan, we don't want to miss anything!"

Little-friend-Susan grabbed her change and the package, and said "Thank you" to Miss Muggins, and they ran along as fast as they could go, and squeezed in among the people looking on in front of the Inn.

A deep voice growled down at them suddenly: "Now, then! Who are you trying to push over?"

THEY SQUEEZED IN AMONG THE PEOPLE

And it was Mr Rudge the Blacksmith, in his dirty leather apron! He put out his big arm and scooped them both round to the front of him, where they could see beautifully. Only there wasn't much to see, and there was a rope to keep people from getting too close.

There were some men in raincoats and woollen scarves talking together. And there was a big sort of camera on one side, and a sort of engine-thing with wires coming from it which people kept nearly tripping over. Billy Blunt was standing close to this, staring at it with his hands in his pockets.

Milly-Molly-Mandy edged over and said to him: "Hullo, Billy! What are they doing? Have we missed a lot?"

Billy Blunt said: "No. They only stand and talk. This thing's for making floodlight come on. Can't think why they don't get on and use it."

A man with rather long hair was walking about, holding a lot of papers in one hand and stroking his hair back with the other. He looked very busy, but he didn't seem to do anything exactly. By the Inn door were two or three children whom Milly-Molly-Mandy didn't know, and a woman knitting on a camp-stool.

Little-friend-Susan said: "I wonder why they are allowed up close and not us. It's not fair."

Then they saw Miss Muggins' Jilly playing on the grass just on the other side of the rope (where she oughtn't to have been). Milly-Molly-Mandy called to her:

"Jilly, your aunty says it'll be your dinner-time soon, and don't you be late!"

Miss Muggins' Jilly waved back and nodded till her curls flapped. But she didn't go.

Billy Blunt said to Milly-Molly-Mandy:

"See that old man on the bench there? He isn't old. He's acting. You have to watch him. Expect I'll have to go home soon."

"So ought we, I expect," said Milly-Molly-Mandy. "Only we don't want to miss anything. When are they going to begin?"

"Huh!" said Billy Blunt. "Not till next year, this rate."

The Blacksmith said: "Well, I've had all I want. I'd rather go the cinema and see things moving!" And he went off home.

Just then a man near the camera shouted

out, "Hi, you!" and
waved his hand at
Miss Muggins' Jilly.
It did rather look at
first as if he were
beckoning – and
Miss Muggins' Jilly
started hopefully
towards him. But
he was waving her back,
and she had to go behind the
rope again, very disappointed.

And then a man held up a sort of black-
and-white signboard, and the woman who
was knitting took her stool and got out of
the way. But the children began playing by
the Inn door, and nobody ordered them off.

The old man on the bench folded his hands on his stick as if he didn't know anything was going on. But he didn't look as if he were acting.

The men in raincoats round the camera talked together and pointed here and there, but the children still went on playing their silly sort of tag-game by the steps. (Of course! they were actor-children, Milly-Molly-Mandy could see now.)

And then suddenly everybody stopped and just stood around, and some of the men in raincoats took sandwiches out of their pockets and bit them.

"Is that all?" said little-friend-Susan.

"Practising," said Billy Blunt.

"We ought to go home," said Milly-

Molly-Mandy. "They'll be expecting us."

"Yes, we ought," said little-friend-Susan, "or we'll be late."

"I shall come back directly after my dinner," said Billy Blunt.

"So shall I!" said little-friend-Susan.

And Milly-Molly-Mandy said: "Let's hurry so we can get back quickly."

It was hard to leave, but they did. Milly-Molly-Mandy called to Miss Muggins' Jilly as they went: "You'd better hurry, Jilly, and come back after!"

But Miss Muggins' Jilly didn't want to hear. She was pretending she hadn't meant to throw her little ball so near to the camera, and was trying to get it back.

Milly-Molly-Mandy ran all the way

home, and ate her dinner in record time. And then Father and Mother and Grandpa and Grandma and Uncle and Aunty excused her, and she ran all the way back to the village, joining little-friend-Susan on the way. Billy Blunt was there before them, but, of course, he lived quite near.

And now it really looked as if things were beginning to happen.

The old man was on the Inn bench, and the children playing by the steps again. And now a shabby little car came driving up, and a pretty girl with very pale hair (Milly-Molly-Mandy had never seen her before) came running out and got in beside the nice young man who was driving, and they drove off. (But the car only went round to the other side and stopped.)

Then the very big, shiny car which had passed Milly-Molly-Mandy and little-friend-Susan on the road came driving up very importantly, and almost before it stopped a man jumped out and ran up the steps. He called out something to the old man on the bench which the old man didn't seem to understand, but the children pointed where the other car had driven away (though it was just standing on the other side now). The man jumped into the big, shiny car again, and it slid off very fast. (Only it too only went round to the other side and stopped.)

And then the men in raincoats (only most of them were in shirt-sleeves now) began talking together and pointing here and there. And suddenly they pointed to where Milly-Molly-Mandy and little-friend-Susan and Billy Blunt were standing. It did rather look as if they were beckoning, but Milly-Molly-Mandy and little-friend-Susan and Billy Blunt took care to keep well back, though they were behind the rope, anyhow.

But one of the men came walking towards them over the grass. And he said:

"I say, would you three care to come and help swell the ranks? We want to see how it looks with a few more youngsters in the picture."

WOULD they!

Milly-Molly Mandy and little-friend-

Susan and (after a moment) Billy Blunt too followed the man to the front of the movie-camera, feeling rather nervous but frightfully excited. (And wouldn't you have been?)

They were put rather behind the other children (who, of course, were Real Actors, and had paint on their faces when you saw them close to). The man told them to look at the cars as they came up, and to be sure never, NEVER, so much as to glance at the camera. "Not if you value your skins, do you hear?" said the man, sounding quite fierce. (But I think he had a twinkle in his eye.)

Then it was all tried out over again, with the two cars, and the pretty girl coming down the steps as before, for more practice.

Then there was some shouting, and everybody who wasn't in the film was got out of the way. (But Milly-Molly-Mandy and little-friend-Susan and Billy Blunt didn't have to move!)

Somebody shouted, "Action!" and the children started playing again, and Milly-Molly-Mandy and little-friend-Susan and Billy Blunt didn't look at the camera. The first car came up, and the other car came up, and the actor-children pointed the way which the first car went. And all the time Milly-Molly-Mandy and little-friend-Susan and Billy Blunt didn't once glance round at the camera.

Then suddenly it was all over, and the man who first spoke to them shook hands with all three, and thanked them for coming to help.

And they went back to their side of the rope again.

And at that moment Miss Muggins' poor Jilly (who did so want to act in the pictures!) came hurrying up –
just in time to see
them coming away
from in front of the
camera.

"Did they let you
act in the film? Oh,
why didn't you call
me too?" wailed Miss
Muggins' Jilly.

"But you weren't

anywhere about," said Milly-Molly-Mandy.

"I expect they'd have let you come, only you went home so late," said little-friend-Susan.

Billy Blunt grinned at Miss Muggins' Jilly.

"You'd better not be late to dinner next time if you want to be a film-star like us!" he said. "I tell you what, though," he added grandly, "you can have my autograph for your album!"

Miss Muggins' Jilly hadn't got an autograph album, and she didn't want Billy Blunt's autograph anyhow! But it gave her an idea. She ran back for pencil and paper, and managed to get the man who sat on the bench and two of the actor-children to write their names for her before they went away. And having three real film-actors' autographs, she thought, was next best to acting in a film herself!

It was a long while before the picture came to the next village where the cinema was. And, of course, everybody had to go and see it then.

But the part that Milly-Molly-Mandy and little-friend-Susan and Billy Blunt acted in was over so quickly you couldn't really recognize them. But if you were looking at the right spot you might happen to notice a bit of Milly-Molly-Mandy's striped frock.

Still, everyone in the village felt quite proud of Billy Blunt, little-friend-Susan, and Milly-Molly-Mandy!

7

Milly-Molly-Mandy and Guy Fawkes Day

Once upon a time Milly-Molly-Mandy and some of the others were coming home from school one afternoon. It was getting dusk, and fallen leaves were chasing each other along the road.

When they came to Miss Muggins' shop Milly-Molly-Mandy and little-friend-Susan and Billy Blunt stopped a moment to look in Miss Muggins' shop-window. Miss Muggins' shop mostly sold uninteresting things, like stockings and dusters and baby-clothes. But it sold some interesting things too, like sweets and toys and pencil-cases. So it was worth looking in sometimes to see if there was anything worth looking at.

And – do you know! – there *was* something! There was a bright-pink cardboard face with slits for eyes, and a box full of blue and red sticks and curly things of odd sizes. And directly Milly-Molly-Mandy and little-friend-Susan and Billy Blunt saw them they said loudly and all together: "Oh! It's Guy Fawkes!" They weren't sure when the Fifth of November was, but of course it must be soon, what with the dark afternoons and the fallen leaves and those things in Miss Muggins' shop window.

"We ought to have a guy with a horrid face on it!" said Milly-Molly-Mandy.

"We ought to have a big bonfire and dance round it!" said little-friend-Susan.

"We ought to buy some fireworks," said Billy Blunt.

"Let's start saving our pocket-money and collecting things for Guy Fawkes day!" said Milly-Molly-Mandy.

So, to begin with, they all went along together to the nice white cottage with the thatched roof (where Milly-Molly-Mandy lived) for Milly-Molly-Mandy to ask if they

THERE WAS A BRIGHT-PINK CARDBOARD FACE

might start making a bonfire out in the yard for Guy Fawkes night.

Father said: "Go ahead. I'll be sawing some dead branches off the big walnut-tree soon, which you can have for it."

Mother said: "Here's an old hat of Father's which looks about right for a guy!"

Grandpa said: "I've torn my old raincoat on the gate and I'm afraid it's past mending now. You'd better have that too."

Grandma said: "Take it, quick, Milly-Molly-Mandy, before he changes his mind. I'm tired of trying to patch it."

Uncle said: "I suppose you'll be wanting some squibs to make me jump. Here's a shilling for you."

Aunty said: "I'll say this for Guy Fawkes

day – it gives you a chance to get rid of the rubbish!" And she handed over a pair of gardening-gloves with the fingers in holes.

Milly-Molly-Mandy and little-friend-Susan and Billy Blunt were very pleased.

They went out into the yard to decide where to have the bonfire, and Billy Blunt carried the old hat and coat and gloves, which were exactly right for a guy. "I'd better take these home and put them in our shed," said Billy Blunt. "They'll be safer there."

Then he and little-friend-Susan had to hurry off to their teas, and Milly-Molly-Mandy went in to hers.

For the next week or so after school they were all very busy collecting firewood. It was quite hard work to find enough for a really big bonfire. They lugged home fallen branches and bundles of twigs and baskets of fir-cones from the woods and hedges. Sometimes they found bits of loose fencing

too, but they knew they mustn't take those, so they always tried to fix them back in place (because, of course, you mustn't let cows and sheep get out to wander on the road or lose themselves).

They clubbed together and bought the horridest pink cardboard face in Miss Muggins' shop, and as many squibs as they could get for their money. Billy Blunt had charge of these (because you could trust Billy Blunt not to let them off before the time). He took charge of making the guy too, as he had its clothes, and he promised to bring it along on the Fifth, ready for the burning.

Soon the bonfire had grown to a fine, great heap, so that only Father or Uncle could add things to it, because nobody else could reach high enough.

And then on Guy Fawkes day – would you believe it! – it *rained*.

Going to school, Milly-Molly-Mandy and little-friend-Susan and Billy Blunt did hope it would stop in time for the bonfire that evening. It wasn't far for little-

friend-Susan to come from the Moggs' cottage, but it was quite a walk for Billy Blunt, right down in the village.

"We wouldn't want to light the bonfire if you couldn't come, Billy," said Milly-Molly-Mandy.

"We'd have to have it tomorrow instead," said little-friend-Susan.

"Wouldn't be Guy Fawkes day tomorrow," said Billy Blunt. (Which was quite true.)

"You've got our fireworks, don't forget," said Milly-Molly-Mandy.

"And our guy, remember," said little-friend-Susan.

"Don't you worry," said Billy Blunt.

But you never knew – mothers often got fussy over your going out on rainy evenings, getting school clothes wet and that sort of thing.

When Milly-Molly-Mandy got home that afternoon she hoped Mother wouldn't notice her wet coat when she took it off. But Mother did. And she hung it up in the kitchen to dry, and her hat and rubber boots too.

"They're sopping, Milly-Molly-Mandy," said Mother. "We shall only just get them dry enough for you to wear to school tomorrow."

Milly-Molly-Mandy's heart sank.

"But what about going out to the bonfire tonight?" she asked.

"We shall have to think about that," said Mother. "Call the others in to tea now, Milly-Molly-Mandy."

During tea (Milly-Molly-Mandy had a little brown egg with hers) she suddenly wondered out loud: "Why do we have Guy Fawkes day, and burn him?"

Father said: "Don't you know? He was a real live person once."

Mother said: "He tried to blow up Parliament with gunpowder years and years ago."

Grandpa said: "Just when the King and important people were coming to open it."

Grandma said: "But they found out just in time, and he and his bad friends were punished."

Uncle said: "And now you kids want to blow us all up with your squibs and bonfires to celebrate him."

Aunty said: "No, it's because they are so glad Parliament was saved!"

"Well," said Milly-Molly-Mandy, sucking her egg-spoon, "I'm glad Guy Fawkes didn't manage to blow up anything. But I don't think I want our guy to be burnt – *he* hasn't done anything naughty!" And then she asked, "Have you thought about what I can wear when we burn the bonfire to-night?"

So directly tea was over Mother got an old jacket of her own and put it on Milly-Molly-Mandy (she had to tuck the cuffs up a lot). And she wrapped an old shawl round Milly-Molly-Mandy's head and shoulders. And she put her own goloshes over Milly-Molly-Mandy's shoes and tied them on with string.

Milly-Molly-Mandy looked like a proper little guy herself!

Then there came a tapping on the back door. And in shuffled little-friend-Susan, in her father's water-proof cape (which came down below her knees) and her mother's rubber boots (which came nearly up to her knees) and her own pixy hood.

Little-friend-Susan looked a proper little guy too!

Even Toby the dog barked at them. (But he wagged his tail too.)

Then both the little guys shuffled outside to look for Billy Blunt. It was dark and wet, but not actually raining now, and it felt very exciting to be out.

"I do hope his mother lets him come,"

said Milly-Molly-Mandy.

"So do I," said little-friend-Susan. "He's got all our things."

But they couldn't see him coming along the road, so they shuffled round to the yard to look at their bonfire.

Father and Uncle were both there with a lantern, and just as they came up Father put a match to a rocket fixed to a fence-post. There was a great *bang!* and a *whoosh!* and showers of beautiful stars lit up everything.

Milly-Molly-Mandy and little-friend-Susan shrieked with excitement, and Milly-Molly-Mandy cried, "Oh, I wish Billy Blunt would come quickly!"

And then, suddenly, they saw the guy!

It was sitting on the bonfire heap – a

splendid guy, with a horrid pink cardboad face, and a dirty old hat and raincoat, and ragged gloves at the end of its stiff, sticking-out arms. Milly-Molly-Mandy and little-friend-Susan shrieked again with excitement, and they looked about everywhere for Billy Blunt (because, of course, they knew the guy couldn't have got there by itself). Uncle hung the lantern on the barn door, and they searched in the barn, and round the cowshed. But they couldn't see Billy Blunt.

"Well," said Father; "we'd better get your bonfire going now, and not wait any longer."

"Oh, don't burn the guy yet!" said Milly-Molly-Mandy. "Let's save it – perhaps Billy Blunt will come."

It looked such a horrid guy, with its pink grinning face. She didn't like to reach up and touch it to push it out of the way. But Uncle said loudly:

"Oh, let's burn it up and get it done with!" And he struck a match.

And then – what DO you think happened?

144

The guy suddenly threw up its tattered gardening-glove hands, and it jumped down off the bonfire to the ground in a great hurry, all by itself!

You should have heard Milly-Molly-Mandy's and little-friend-Susan's shrieks! Then the pink cardboard mask fell off and rolled on the ground, and they saw someone else's face

145

grinning at them under the guy's shabby old hat.

"It's Billy Blunt!" shrieked Milly-Molly-Mandy, catching hold of his ragged old coat.

"It's Billy Blunt!" shrieked little-friend-Susan, picking up the cardboard mask and trying it on herself.

"*Boo!*" shouted Billy Blunt, waving his arms. But he couldn't frighten them any more, now that they knew who it was.

So then he told them how his mother hadn't wanted him to come out and get his school clothes wet again, and how he had taken the old hat and coat off the guy he had made and put them on himself instead. So then Mrs Blunt had let him come along and pretend to be the guy.

"Huh! Frightened you girls properly, didn't I?" said Billy Blunt, grinning, as he handed them their share of squibs out of his coat-pockets.

"You were frightened too, properly, when you thought Uncle was going to light the bonfire!" said Milly-Molly-Mandy.

"Serve you right for frightening us so!" said little-friend-Susan.

Then Uncle really put a match to the bonfire, and it began to blaze up. And Father let off some more rockets. And Grandpa and Grandma and Mother and Aunty came out to watch (leaving Toby the dog and Topsy the cat safely shut indoors, lest they should get scared at the noise and run away). And Milly-Molly-Mandy and little-friend-Susan and Billy Blunt lit their squibs, which cracked and banged and made Uncle jump so much that they laughed and laughed!

And what with the roaring of the bonfire and the banging of the fireworks and the shouts of Milly-Molly-Mandy and little-friend-Susan and Billy Blunt, anyone would know they had a splendid Guy Fawkes celebration, even though they didn't burn the guy.

But that, said Father, was because it was really too difficult to choose, with *three* guys jumping round and round the bonfire!

Anyhow, they burnt the guy's dirty old

hat and gloves. But his raincoat Mrs Blunt had to put into the dustbin as soon as Billy Blunt got home again that evening after the bonfire was out!

About the Author

Joyce Lankester Brisley was born over a hundred years ago, on 6 February 1896. She had two sisters: an elder one, Ethel, and Nina, who was just a year younger than Joyce. The family lived in Bexhill-on-Sea in Sussex, in a house so close to the sea that when there was a very high tide the waves would come right into the garden. Joyce's father ran a chemist's shop in the town. Her mother enjoyed drawing and painting, but had to spend most of her time looking after the home and her children.

Joyce and her sisters were all good at art, like their mother, and went to evening classes at Hastings School of Art, taking the train there and back along the coast. By the time they were teenagers, "Eth" (as Ethel was always known in the family) was having her pictures accepted for exhibitions at the Royal Academy in London and was soon selling paintings as a result. Then, through a friend, the girls were invited to meet Miss Brown of the magazine *Home Chat*. They quickly began to do illustrations for this magazine, so for the first time all three sisters started to earn money for themselves.

This money was soon to become very important for the family. In 1912, when Joyce was sixteen, her parents separated. In her diary (writing in French as if to keep it a secret) she recorded that her father wanted his family to leave the house. They stayed until Joyce and

Nina had finished their term at art school, then the three girls moved with their mother to South London, where Eth had found them a tiny flat.

In London, Joyce and Nina enrolled at the Lambeth School of Art in 1912 – an uncle kindly agreed to pay the fees for both girls. They studied there five days a week for two years. In 1913 they moved to a house with a large room that the three girls could use as a studio.

The outbreak of the First World War in 1914 meant that food was scarce. Their mother had to spend a lot of time searching for meat and vegetables she could afford, while the girls worked hard earning money from illustrations for magazines, newspapers and advertisements. Joyce writes in her diary about drawing advertisements for Cherry Blossom boot polish and Mansion floor polish. She also writes about the German bombing raids on London – describing how, in September 1916, the sisters had to get up in the middle of the night and go downstairs for safety, still in their nightclothes and bedtime plaits.

Despite the war and constant worries about money, family life continued happily throughout this time. In 1917 Joyce records in her diary that Nina (daringly) wanted to cut her hair short, and Eth longed to do the same, but Joyce felt "I couldn't – it wouldn't suit me well at all". The sisters obviously got along very well together, but nevertheless Joyce wished she had some privacy. She was delighted when, shortly after her twenty-first birthday, she was able to have a room of her own – "My longing, for years and years."

In 1918 they all moved again, to a house with

a larger studio. Joyce went with her mother and sisters to the local Christian Science Church. There they met an artist who worked for *The Christian Science Monitor.* As a result, both Joyce and Nina began submitting stories and drawings to the paper, and it was on the Children's Page in October 1925 that the first story about Milly-Molly-Mandy appeared. The idea had come into Joyce's mind one day when "the sun was shining and I longed to be out in the country instead of sitting indoors all day, earning a living . . ."

Milly-Molly-Mandy was an immediate success and soon began to gain a strong following among readers. Joyce records that:

"*. . . boys and girls began writing letters to the paper, to the editors and to Milly-Molly-Mandy herself, wanting to know more about her, asking,*

Could she come for a holiday by the sea? Could she have a baby sister to take out riding in the pram? (She couldn't, as she was an 'only' child, but little-friend-Susan could, and did.) Some of the letters enclosed foreign stamps for Billy Blunt's collection (so generous!). One boy wrote all the way from Australia to tell me that 'Father' was shown digging with his wrong foot on the spade (for it seems the left foot is the right foot for digging with!). I wrote back to thank him and promised to alter the drawing before it went into a book – as you may see I did, for it's nice to get things quite correct."

Joyce went on writing stories about Milly-Molly-Mandy for the rest of her life, but she wrote about other characters too, in books such as *Marigold in Godmother's House* (1934) and *Adventures of Purl and Plain* (1941). She also illustrated stories by other authors and was specially chosen by her publisher, George Harrap, to draw the pictures for the first edition of Ursula Moray Williams's *Adventures of the Little Wooden Horse* (1938).

Joyce always remained close to her sisters. Nina, who became the first and much-loved illustrator of the Chalet School stories by Elinor M. Brent-Dyer, was the only one to marry. Ethel died in 1961, and Nina and Joyce died within a few months of each other, in 1978.

Joyce Lankester Brisley seems to have been rather a shy person and she obviously didn't like publicity. Once, after two of her pictures had been accepted by the Royal Academy and a journalist wanted to interview her, she telegraphed at once that she "would be out". Maybe she was a bit like Milly-Molly-Mandy herself – happy to be busily getting on with whatever task or errand she'd set herself for the day, and content with whatever good fortune life might bring her.

Have you read?

Milly-
Molly-
Mandy
Stories

Joyce Lankester Bristley

More of
Milly-
Molly-
Mandy

Joyce Lankester Brisley

Have you read?

Further Doings of
Milly-
Molly-
Mandy

Joyce Lankester Brisley

Have you read?

Milly-
Molly-
Mandy
Again

Joyce Lankester Brisley

Have you read?

Milly-
Molly-
Mandy
and Billy Blunt
Joyce Lankester Brisley

Collect them all!